REBEL

Bob Temple

illustrated by Sean Tiffany

Librarian Reviewer
Chris Kreie, Media Specialist

Reading Consultant
Mary Evenson, Teacher

Raintree

www.raintreepublishers.co.uk
Visit our website to find out
more information about
Raintree books.

To order:
☎ Phone 0845 6044371
🖨 Fax +44 (0) 1865 312263
🖳 Email myorders@capstonepub.co.uk

Customers from outside the UK please telephone +44 1865 312262

Raintree is an imprint of Capstone Global Library Limited, a company incorporated in England and Wales having its registered office at 7 Pilgrim Street, London, EC4V 6LB – Registered company number: 6695582

"Raintree" is a registered trademark of Pearson Education Limited, under licence to Capstone Global Library Limited

Text © Stone Arch Books, 2007
First published in the United Kingdom
by Capstone Global Library in 2010
The moral rights of the proprietor have been asserted.

Edited in the UK by Laura Knowles
Art Director: Heather Kindseth
Graphic Designer: Kay Fraser
Originated by Capstone Global Library
Printed and bound in China by Leo Paper Products Ltd

ISBN 978 1 406213 74 4 (hardback)
14 13 12 11 10
10 9 8 7 6 5 4 3 2 1

ISBN 978 1 406213 95 9 (paperback)
14 13 12 11 10
10 9 8 7 6 5 4 3 2 1

British Library Cataloguing in Publication Data
Temple, Bob.
Board rebel. -- (Sport stories)
813.6-dc22
A full catalogue record for this book is available from the British Library.

Disclaimer
All the Internet addresses (URLs) given in this book were valid at the time of going to press. However, due to the dynamic nature of the Internet, some addresses may have changed, or sites may have changed or ceased to exist since publication. While the author and publishers regret any inconvenience this may cause readers, no responsibility for any such changes can be accepted by either the author or the publishers.

CONTENTS

Chapter 1

King of the Park

Mason Jenkins tipped the front edge of his skateboard over the lip of the ramp. His back foot held the board in place by its tail. His front foot tapped at the battered front edge of the board.

Mason looked down at the board. All the slides and grinds he had done over the last year had left his board in bad shape. "Time for a new one," he thought. "But I'm sure that won't happen until my birthday."

Two more months. It would be hard to wait. It might even be harder for him to part with the board that helped him win his first Citywide Skateboard Challenge, however.

Mason's eyes scanned over the other, younger skaters as they whipped around the park. The younger kids rode back and forth between the smallest ramps.

Mason smiled. It wasn't that long ago that he was one of those little kids. Now he was standing at the top of the biggest half-pipe in the city.

"Hey, Mason, what are you waiting for?" came a voice from the other end of the pipe. It was Billy Collins, one of Mason's best skateboarding mates. "Let's see what you've got up your sleeve today!"

Mason grinned. "A lot more than you, that's for sure," he called.

With that, he tipped the board forward and rode it down the ramp. He was heading straight for Billy, who was standing at the top of the opposite side of the ramp. Mason's grin grew as his board climbed the far edge of the pipe.

Mason barrelled off the top edge of the pipe. He flew up, turned a perfect three-sixty in front of Billy's face, and dropped easily back down into the half-pipe. "Beat that!" Mason called back to Billy.

Billy laughed, then jumped down the half-pipe, trailing after Mason. They spent the rest of the day chasing each other and trying out new tricks. Each boy would try something new, and the other would quickly try to match it.

By the end of the day, they were pretty tired and really sore. Even with all of their protective gear on, they still came away with some bumps and bruises. Mason's trousers, already ripped up from a number of falls, had some new damage.

Finally, it was time to head home. Mason and Billy headed off together, grinding on curbs and jumping over cracks in the pavement and anything else they could find. A couple of roads away from Mason's house, Billy turned down a different street. "Catch you later," he said.

"You'll never catch me," Mason said, laughing.

Mason wheeled for home. He was still the best skater at the park. But he didn't know about the surprise that was waiting for him at home.

Chapter 2

The Big Surprise

Mason wheeled around to the back of the house. He flipped his board up into his right hand, swung the back door open, and walked inside.

"Mason? Is that you?" his dad called from the kitchen. "Come in here, quick! We've got a big surprise for you!"

At last! Mason thought to himself. They finally decided to get me a new skateboard!

Mason turned the corner and walked into the kitchen. He glanced around the room quickly.

There was no new skateboard that he could see. But both of his parents smiled broadly at him. Mason stood in the doorway.

Something was up. Normally, food would be getting cooked and his parents would be asking him about his day.

Instead, they just looked at him, smiling. "What's going on?" Mason asked. "You're both acting, um, weird."

"We've got big news," Mason's dad said. "I'm getting promoted at work."

"Oh, cool," Mason said.

"Mason," his mum said. "This is really good news. Your dad worked hard for this."

"Oh, I know," Mason said. He struggled to sound more excited about it. "I mean, that's great. Good job, Dad." Mason felt uncomfortable. He tried to leave the room.

"Mason, wait," his mum said. "There's more. Dad's going to be working in a different office," she said. "Out in Woodbury. Near my office."

"Oh, that's cool," Mason said to his mum. "You'll have company on the drive."

Again, Mason turned to leave. Finally, his parents couldn't hold it in any more.

"Um, Mason," his mum said, "it's not going to be a long drive."

There was a pause. Mason started to realize that he might not like what was coming next.

"We're moving," his dad said.

Chapter 3

It seemed like Mason had no time to get ready. In just a month, the house had been sold and he was moving. He could hardly believe it was happening.

Woodbury was only an hour away. It might have been a million miles to Mason. He wouldn't be close to his friend Billy. He wouldn't be close to the city skate park he loved. He wouldn't be close to anyone he knew.

His parents bought a fancy new house in a very nice neighbourhood.

It was nothing like what Mason was used to. The new house had three floors. Mason's bedroom was about twice as big as his old bedroom.

There was a separate room that his parents had set up as a games room for Mason. It had a big-screen TV for computer games and a pool table.

Mason's parents put the family computer in that room too. Mason knew he'd spend a lot of time in there.

The best part of the new house was in the back garden. It was a giant swimming pool.

On the night they moved in, Mason turned on his computer.

When he discovered Billy was online, he sent him an instant message.

"U wouldn't believe my new house," Mason wrote.

"Big?" Billy wrote back.

"It's ace," Mason wrote. "Pool and games room. You should come see it."

"Lucky," Billy wrote.

Mason wasn't so sure. True, his new surroundings were nothing like his old neighbourhood. But that was part of the problem. Mason didn't quite feel comfortable in the new neighbourhood.

Every day after school, Mason hopped on his skateboard and explored the area. He rode up and down the streets. He grinded on the curbs. He practiced his kick flips and his one-eighties.

There was no skate park to be found. What he did find were beautiful lawns and perfect flower gardens. Worse, some of the pavements were made of stone. That made it very hard to skateboard.

Near some of the shops in town, he found some steps and railings he could use to do tricks. When he tried to do them during the day, however, the shop owners told him to stop.

Mason was lonely. Instant-messaging with Billy wasn't helping either.

"There was a new kid at the park today," Billy wrote one night. "He was pretty good."

"Nobody here skates," Mason wrote. After three weeks, Mason hadn't made any friends.

Chapter 4

One night after dinner, the doorbell rang. Mason got up from the computer and headed towards the steps.

When he reached the top of the stairs, he saw that his mum had already answered the door. She was talking to a woman in a fancy dress. Mason recognized her.

The woman lived down the street. One day when Mason was skateboarding, the woman had yelled at him.

She'd told him to stay off her property.

Mason was pretty sure that her visit wasn't to welcome them to the neighbourhood.

Mason tried to listen, but he couldn't hear everything.

"It's got to stop," he heard the woman say. "The vote was unanimous."

Mason's mom was nice to the woman, but Mason could tell she was not happy. She invited the woman in, but the woman said she was on her way to a concert.

When the woman left, Mason came down the stairs.

"What's she talking about, Mum?" Mason said.

Mason's mum looked sad. "Well, we've got a little problem," she said.

"Let's go into the living room and talk about it as a family."

Mason didn't like the sound of that, either. It had to be bad news.

"That was Mrs Parsons," Mason's mum said. "She's the chairperson of our neighborhood committee."

"Yeah?" Mason said. "So what?"

"She said that the committee is upset with the marks that your skateboard leaves on the curbs and pavements," Mason's mum said. "And the shop managers are upset about you riding the railings by the shopping area."

"Too bad for them," Mason said. "It's a free country."

"That's true, but we all have to live by the rules," Mason's dad said.

"What does that mean?" Mason asked.

"It means that we all agree to follow the rules that the neighbourhood committee makes," Mason's mum said. "Unfortunately, at their meeting tonight, they agreed to a new rule."

"What's that?" Mason asked.

"No skateboarding on the town's streets," his mum said.

Chapter 5

Finding the Curves

The next morning, Mason woke up feeling determined. He strapped his skateboard on the back of his bike and set off.

He wasn't going to return until he found a place to skateboard – a place where no one could tell him he couldn't.

His plan was to get outside the town of Woodbury. He hoped that a neighbouring city might be less strict about its rules.

He didn't have to go very far. About a kilometre away, he came across a park.

He knew he was still in Woodbury, but the park looked like a great place to skate. There were curving, paved paths winding all around.

"It's still in Woodbury," he thought. "But these paths aren't town streets. They can't stop me from skateboarding here."

Then he saw it.

On the far left side of the park, there was a large hill. From top to bottom, the hill featured a long, winding path. It was perfectly paved, with a mixture of sharp, hairpin turns and big downhill drops. The path wound its way through a flower garden with a fountain and a statue of somebody old and famous.

Mason could imagine the adults in the city taking long, slow walks through this beautiful park in the evenings. On a nice summer weekday like this one, however, the paths were empty. A few small children played in the playground area with a parent, but no one was using the paths.

In a flash, Mason rode his bike to the highest point of the path. He stood there, straddling his bike, wondering if he dared try to ride down the sloping path.

From the top, parts of the path looked more like cliffs. Every turn looked more dangerous and exciting than the one before it.

Mason swung his right leg off his bike. He quickly began untying his skateboard from the back. Then he heard a voice.

"Hey, kid."

Mason wheeled around. There were three boys approaching from behind him. They were all neatly dressed. Mason wondered what they thought of him in his ripped jeans and scruffy T-shirt.

"What do you think you are doing?" said the tall one in the middle.

Mason pushed his brown curls away from his eyes. "What's it to you?" he said.

The three boys walked up to Mason. None of them smiled. The middle one took off his rucksack and set it aside.

Mason wasn't worried about a fight. They were dressed too smartly to get dirty. He looked at the middle boy's rucksack. Monogrammed on the front pocket were the initials "BP".

"This is our park, that's what," the middle one said. "Where do you live?"

"Just over there," Mason said, pointing in the direction of his house. "About a kilometre from here. We just moved in."

"You must be that skateboarder who's got everybody mad," the boy said. "You've got a few things to learn about Woodbury."

"Like what?" Mason asked.

"Like nobody skateboards here," he said.

"Well," Mason said, "I do."

"Not down the Curves, you don't," the boy said.

"The Curves?" Mason said. "So it has a name, huh? Are you telling me no one's ever skateboarded down the Curves?"

"That's right," the boy said. "And you won't either."

"Sorry," Mason said, "you're wrong about that, too."

Mason was on his skateboard and on his way down the hill before anyone could move. The first few turns were easy. As he careened down the hill, he picked up speed. He was fine on the first few turns, but he found himself getting closer to the edges with each corner.

The final turn was the hardest. It was a sharp turn. Mason leaned in hard as he made the turn. He stretched his arms out and bent his knees to help keep his balance.

His back wheels wobbled. Mason wavered, but stayed up on the board. Finally, he reached the last straightaway. He pumped his fist above his head.

It was the first time he had felt good about his new home.

Chapter 6

Benjamin Parsons

Despite the long uphill walk to the top of the Curves, Mason's smile never left his face. The three boys at the top were smiling too.

"Not bad," the one in the middle said. "I'm Benjamin Parsons."

Suddenly, Mason knew what "BP" on the rucksack meant. "This is Will," Benjamin said, gesturing to the boy on the left. "And this is Angus."

"Hi," Mason said, nodding to the boys. There was an uncomfortable pause, then Mason spoke up. "So, none of you guys skateboard?"

Will started to answer, but Benjamin interrupted. "Ah, no," he scoffed. "We don't. Better things to do."

"Whatever you say, BP," Mason said. "But you're missing out."

"The name is Benjamin," he said. "No one calls me anything but Benjamin."

"Okay," Mason said. Mason fiddled with his skateboard. He tugged at a little sliver of wood that was falling off one edge.

The three boys huddled briefly. Then Benjamin spoke up.

"That was a pretty good ride," he said. "You should try the railings."

Mason glanced down the hill. About halfway down the Curves, in between two of the hairpin switchbacks, was a small stone staircase. The steps went right between the fountain and the statue.

Alongside the steps were two sets of railings. There was about a one metre gap between the railings.

"It would be pretty cool to see you do the Curves and the rails," Benjamin said. "If you can do that, you might be able to fit in around here."

Mason eyed the challenge. He knew it wouldn't be easy. "I'm not interested in fitting in around here," Mason said. "But I'll do it anyway."

Benjamin and Angus grinned. Mason knew they wanted him to blow it.

Then Mason caught Will's eye. Will looked worried.

Mason smiled. "Tell you what, BP," he said. Benjamin's grin disappeared. "If I make it down the rails, how about you give it a try?"

Benjamin rolled his eyes. "Fine," he said.

Mason took off. He found the going easier on the turns this time. He learned from his first trip down, and this second ride was much smoother. He kept his eyes focused on the rails as they grew nearer.

Mason cut a sharp turn to the left, crossing back. One turn remained before the rails. He braced himself as he turned back right.

He got ready for the jump up to the first rail. He'd done rails a million times.

But he had never done it at this speed, and he'd never done it on this steep an incline.

Mason pumped down on his board and popped it up as he leaped for the first rail. He went for a front-side board slide. The front wheels would go over the rail, and the middle of his board would slide down the rail.

Mason's left foot was forward. He would take the first rail facing the top of the hill, then try a one-eighty turn and take the second rail down.

The board seemed to stick to the bottom of his feet. It looked perfect. Mason popped up on the first rail.

"Wow!" Will exclaimed. Benjamin shot him an angry glance.

Mason felt a rush of confidence. He had nailed it. He eyed the boys at the top of the hill and gave them a little grin. When he looked back to the rail, however, the gap was approaching faster than he thought.

His legs pumped to try to get some air so he could cover the gap. But he was too late. The board was already coming off the first rail, and he didn't get the push he needed to make it to the second one.

As he tried to make the one-eighty turn, his left foot slipped off the board. Now he was spinning, falling, crashing. His left ankle smacked into the railing. The board bounced off the rail and hit him in the face. He tried to grab the rail with his arm but missed.

He landed hard in the flowerbed, but he was going too fast to stop quickly.

He tumbled through roses and tulips before a thick shrub snagged him just in time to keep him from hitting the next section of the paved path.

Mason lay on his stomach, motionless. His ankle throbbed. He was scraped and bruised and battered. He was bleeding from tiny punctures and scrapes from the thorns on the rose bushes.

Mason rolled to his back and looked to the top of the hill.

The boys were gone.

Chapter 7

That night, as Mason's mum plucked thorns from the rose bushes out of Mason's arms and legs, the doorbell rang. Mason's dad went to the door. Mason couldn't hear the conversation, but he did know who his dad was talking to: Mrs Parsons.

"That didn't take long," Mason muttered.

"What do you mean?" Mason's mum said.

"I'm sure BP Three went straight home and told his mummy what happened," Mason said.

"Mason!" his mum said. "I'm surprised at you. That boy may have egged you on, but you're the one who tried it."

Mason's head sank. He knew she was right. It didn't really matter to him, though. To Mason, the day's events were just more proof that he didn't belong in this neighbourhood. Then his dad came in with the news.

"Well, Mason," his dad said, "they've banned skateboarding in the park, too. And they gave me a bill for the repairs."

Mason stood up, his shoulders slumped, and wandered up the stairs towards his bedroom.

The next morning, Mason's dad greeted him with a surprise. "Hey, Mason, get up and get dressed," he said. "I need to run back to the old neighbourhood. I'll drop you at the skate park if you like."

Mason was out of bed like a shot. The bumps and bruises from the day before still ached, but he pretended not to notice. In just a few minutes, he had his clothes on and his skateboard in his hand, and was headed out the door.

The drive to the park seemed to take forever. Mason couldn't wait. When they arrived at the park, Mason leapt out of the car. "I'll be back at four," his dad said. "That's six hours."

"Okay, Dad!" Mason replied. He dropped his board to the ground and rolled off to the park. "See you."

Mason could see Billy at the half-pipe. He skated over there as fast as he could. Billy tipped over the edge and started down the pipe before he heard Mason.

"Yo, Billy," Mason shouted. "Let's see what you can do today!"

Billy was so shocked that he lost his balance at the bottom of the half-pipe and fell off his board.

"Not much, by the look of it!" Mason said.

Billy wasn't hurt. "Hey, mate!" Billy said. "What are you doing here? Are you moving back?"

"I wish," Mason said. They bumped fists and headed up towards the top of the half-pipe. Mason explained that he was just dropping by for the day.

Off they went. They tracked each other, trying new tricks and challenging each other.

In the middle of the afternoon, Mason noticed another boy about his age across the park. "That's the new kid," Billy said. "He's only here on weekends. He's kind of quiet, but he seems okay."

Something was familiar about the boy, Mason thought. It was hard to tell in the helmet and pads, but he thought he might know him. There was no question he was a good skater. Everything he tried looked very natural. As the boy got closer, Mason caught a glimpse of his face.

"Holy cow," Mason said as the boy approached. "It's you!"

Chapter 8

A New Plan

"Will, right?" Mason said to the boy. He nodded.

"You're BP's friend," Mason said. He stuck out his hand. "I'm Mason," he said. "What are you doing around here?"

"My parents split up, and my dad lives around here," Will said. "So I'm here every weekend."

"I thought kids from Woodbury don't stoop to skateboarding." Mason smirked.

Will smiled. "Some of us like to skateboard. But there are some people who don't like it."

Mason knew who Will meant — the Parsons family. "They pretty much run the whole neighbourhood," Will said. "But Benjamin's cool, once you get to know him."

"I don't think that's going to happen," Mason said. "Not after yesterday."

"That was a cool run," Will said. "Until you biffed, that is."

They both laughed. "Billy and I do this game where we try to match each other's tricks," Mason said. "Want to try?"

Will nodded, and off they went. For the next several hours, the boys matched each other trick for trick at the half-pipe, the rails, the ramps, everywhere.

As four o'clock approached, Mason saw his father pulling up to the park. It was time to go.

"That was fun," Will said. "Thanks."

"No problem," Mason said. "You Woodbury guys aren't so bad after all."

Will laughed. "I just wish the new kid hadn't ruined it for the rest of us in Woodbury," he joked. "Now the only place you can skateboard is your own back garden." Will and Billy laughed, but Mason didn't.

"I was just kidding," Will said. "No reason to get mad."

"No, I'm not mad," Mason said. "What you just said gave me an idea."

Chapter 9

Mason outlined his idea to Will and Billy. They both liked it, but Billy wasn't sure that Mason could pull it off.

"There's no way your dad will say yes," Billy said. "But if he does, count me in."

"Can't hurt to try!" Mason said. "I'll see you guys later."

Mason headed off to the car. He popped his skateboard into the boot and got into the front seat.

"How was it? Did you have fun with all your old friends?" Mason's dad asked.

"Yeah, it was great," Mason said. "And a boy from Woodbury was there. He comes here on weekends. His dad lives here."

They drove quietly for a while. Mason tried to work out a way to explain his idea to his dad. It was a big idea, one that would be tough to convince a parent to do. Mason thought he needed to ask the question just the right way.

For Mason, there was only one way to do it. He'd have to make a joke out of it.

"Dad," he began, "you know I love our pool, right? Well, I think I'd love it even more if it were . . ."

There was a pause. Even Mason wasn't sure if he could say the next word.

"What?" his dad said. "If it were what? Bigger? Deeper?"

"No," Mason said. "I think I'd love it even more if it were empty."

"What are you talking about?" Mason's dad asked with a laugh.

"I want to have some of the guys over and have a trick contest in your pool," Mason said. "With our skateboards."

"Hmm," his dad said. There was a long silence. "Interesting."

Mason made every promise he could think of. They could fill it back up when it was over. They wouldn't wreck the pool edges. He would help pay for the water to refill it. Everything.

"Okay, okay, settle down," Mason's dad said. "Let me talk to your mum about it."

That night, Mason's parents took him out by the pool. The water level was already about a foot lower than normal. Mason knew what that meant.

"Well, your birthday is coming up," Mason's mum said. "We thought it could be a birthday party."

"This is going to be awesome!" Mason yelled.

Chapter 10

The Big Day

Mason didn't waste any time spreading the news. He told Will to tell kids in Woodbury who wanted to skateboard. Will said he'd bring five or six kids.

"That's great," Mason said. "Just make sure there aren't too many. My parents said no more than ten." Mason felt a little funny about having a party with kids he didn't know. They'd have one thing in common though, and it was skateboarding.

When the day of the party arrived, Mason woke up early. He spent the entire morning making sure everything was just right. The pool was completely empty and ready. The snacks were all ready and the drinks were in the fridge.

Now all he needed was some people.

Billy was the first to arrive. His parents drove him up from the old neighbourhood. Will came a few minutes later. He had three boys and a girl with him. But no Benjamin. Mason took them into the back garden. "Where's my old pal BP?" he joked. "I'm surprised he's not here!"

"I didn't tell him about it," Will said. "I was afraid he'd be mad at me for coming."

Soon, the kids were zipping up and down the walls of the pool.

At first, the Woodbury kids were a little shaky. Some of them didn't skateboard much, and they didn't want to try anything too risky.

Mason and Billy showed them how to do some simple tricks. Before long, they were flying around, trying one-eighties and even harder tricks. They hooted for one another's great moves and helped each other when they fell.

After a while, Mason sat down on the patio and took in the scene. "Looks like you made some friends," his mum said. She smiled. "Are we ever going to have a swimming pool again, or is this a skate park now?"

"We'll have a pool again," Mason said, "because we're going to have a skate park in Woodbury before I'm done."

"I don't know about that one," Mason's mum said. "You'd have to convince the committee, and that won't be easy."

"I know," Mason said.

"Speaking of the committee," Mason's mum said, "where is that Parsons boy?"

"He doesn't like me much," Mason said. "Will didn't even tell him about the party."

"That's weird," his mum said. "I could have sworn I saw him outside the fence holding a skateboard a little while ago. I thought he was on his way around to the back gate."

Chapter 11

Finding BP

Mason jumped up. He ran for the back gate and went out. No one was there.

"Are you sure you saw him?" he asked his mother.

"Yes," she said. "Maybe you and Will should go look for him."

Mason grabbed Will and told him what happened. They headed towards Benjamin's house. As they turned the corner to the park, they couldn't believe what they saw.

There, at the top of the Curves, was Benjamin Parsons. He had a skateboard! Will started to call out, but Mason stopped him. "Shh," Mason said. "Let's see what he does."

The boys stayed hidden by a bush. At the top of the hill, Benjamin rocked the board back and forth, taking deep breaths.

He looked ready. Then he stepped up on the skateboard and started down the Curves. He wobbled a little before he even reached the first turn. But around the first turn he went.

Slowly, Benjamin made his way down the Curves. A couple of times he slowed the board so much that he nearly stopped. But he never fell, and the last few turns, he took pretty quickly. When he reached the final straightaway, he pumped a fist in the air, just as Mason had done.

Chapter 12

Suddenly, Mason and Will saw
Benjamin a little differently from how they
had before. They broke out from behind
the bush and cheered.

"Yeah!" Will said. "Woo-hoo!"

"Way to go, BP!" Mason yelled. "That
was awesome!"

Benjamin stopped cold. "What are you
two clowns doing here?" he asked.

"Oh, relax," Mason said. "You were at my house, so we came looking for you."

"I didn't know you could skateboard," Will said excitedly.

"Yeah, and I didn't know you were cool," Mason joked.

"I don't skateboard," Benjamin said.

Mason laughed. "Um, I think you just did!" he said.

"Well, I wanted to try it," Benjamin said. "I did it. Now I'm done."

"Man," Mason said, shaking his head. "You have to learn to lighten up."

"Come back to the party with us," Will said. "It's a blast."

Benjamin thought about it for a second.

"Well," he said, "it did sound like you guys were having fun back there."

Benjamin returned to the party with the boys. He wasn't ready to use the deep end of the pool like a half-pipe.

But he did start out in the shallow end and go back and forth a little bit.

As the day went on, Benjamin started to loosen up.

He learned that skateboarding was really pretty fun, especially once you got good enough to try a few tricks.

"Having fun?" Mason asked Benjamin late in the day.

"Yeah," Benjamin said. "This is great."

"It's even better when you're at a real skate park," Mason said.

He had a little gleam in his eye. "We should see if we can get one built here in Woodbury."

"Fat chance," Benjamin said.

"Why not?" Mason said. "There's plenty of room over near the Curves. And if we all had a place we were allowed to skate, we wouldn't have to skate anywhere else."

"Good point," Benjamin said. "Hmm, let me think."

* * *

Benjamin and Mason spent the next few weeks launching their plan to raise money and convince the committee to build a skate park in Woodbury.

Mason knew it wouldn't be easy to get the committee to agree. But with Benjamin on his side, he thought he had a chance.

In the meantime, he made some plans with his friends, both new and old.

"Hey, Mason," Will said. "My dad said you can stay with us on weekends if you want. Then you can skate at your old neighbourhood park!"

"Great!" Mason replied. "And when my new neighbourhood park is ready, we can skate there too!"

About the Author

Bob Temple has written more than thirty books for children. Over the years, he has coached more than twenty kids' football, basketball, and baseball teams. He also loves visiting classrooms to talk about his writing.

About the Illustrator

When Sean Tiffany was growing up, he lived on a small island. Every day, he had to take a boat to get to school. When Sean isn't working on his art, he works on a multimedia project called "OilCan Drive", which combines music and art. He has a pet cactus named Jim.

Glossary

ally someone who's on your side

challenge something that is hard or requires extra work

committee a small group of people who make decisions for a larger group

confidence having a strong belief in yourself

convince to make another person or group of people believe or agree with you

covenant an agreement or promise to do something

manicured when something is trimmed perfectly

motionless not moving

promoted moved into a new, more important job

protective guarding a person or thing to keep it safe

180 – a turn in which the skateboarder starts out facing one way, and makes a half-circle in the air

360 – a turn in which the skateboarder makes a complete turn in the air

Grind – to ride the skateboard along a surface, such as a curb or railing, by having it slide on the bottom of the board instead of the wheels

Halfpipe – a skateboarding surface with two curved ramps that face each other, connected by a flat surface. Above each ramp is a landing deck.

Kickflip – a trick in which the skateboarder flips the skateboard over and lands back on it

Ollie – a trick in which the skateboarder leaps up into the air, and the skateboard appears to cling to his or her feet

Ramp – an inclined surface for skateboarding

Tail – the back end of the skateboard

Discussion Questions

1. How could Mason have tried harder to fit in to his new neighbourhood at first?

2. Mason likes to be a smart aleck. Can you think of some times in this story when he shouldn't have acted that way?

3. What reasons should Mason and Benjamin use to convince the committee to build a skate park in Woodbury?

4. When Benjamin challenged Mason to ride the rails at The Curves, why do you think Mason agreed?

Writing Prompts

1. If a new person moved into your neighbourhood, how would you treat them? How would you try to make them feel welcome?

2. In this story, Mason had to adjust to living in a new town. Write about a time in your life when you had to adjust to a difficult new situation.

3. Moving away from Billy was hard for Mason. He stayed in touch by using instant messaging. How would you stay connected to your friends if you moved away?

Find Out More

Books

Extreme Skateboarding, Blaine Wiseman
(Weigl Educational Publishers Ltd, 2009)

How to Improve at Skateboarding, Andy
Horsley (ticktock Media, 2009)

Skateboarding Science, Helaine Becker
(Crabtree Publishing Company, 2009)

Websites

www.sk8uk.co.uk/skateboarding-guide
Find out all about how to get started
skateboarding and learn loads of tricks
on this UK skateboarding website.

www.ukskate.org.uk
The United Kingdom Skateboarding
Association website has lots of information
on skateboarding events and competitions.